Dick King-Smith

Emily's *Legs*

Illustrated by Katinka Kew

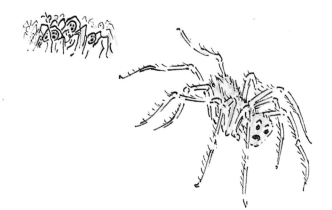

WAYLAND

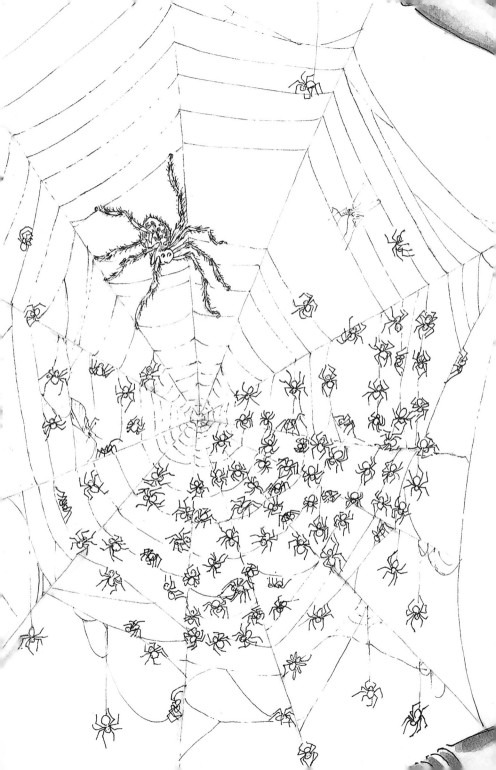

Chapter One

To begin with, nobody noticed.

Mind you, you couldn't blame Mother Spider. If she'd only had one baby, she'd have been sure to notice.

But she had a hundred babies, all hatching out at the same time. How could she be expected to know that ninety-nine spiderlings were normal and one was different?

Father Spider didn't notice. For one thing, he didn't like children.

For another, he was always too busy
sitting quite still, waiting for house-flies
and bluebottles to land in his web, in the
highest darkest corner of the room.

Emily's ninety-nine brothers and sisters
didn't notice.

Nobody noticed, not even Emily, until
the night of the Spider Sports.

For the grown-up spiders, there were lots
of different events. There was web-spinning

(how quickly could you make a whole one from start to finish) and fly-parcelling (how quickly could you tie up a fly in silken threads) and fly-eating (how quickly could you... yes, well, I needn't explain that.

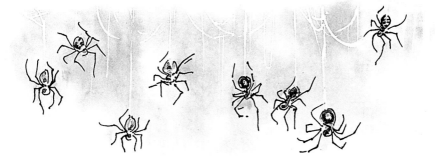

And there was abseiling, where you let out a thread and whizzed down it from the ceiling, and thread-climbing, where you whizzed back up again.

But for the spiderlings there were only the eight-legged races.

Now this was where Emily's troubles began.

Not that she didn't run in the eight-legged races at the Spider Sports.

She did.

Not that she didn't win.

She did.

The trouble was that she won them all and she won them all so easily.

First, all the spiderlings were lined up at one end of the room, and they had to race across the carpet to the other end.

Emily won easily.

Then they had to race up the wall of the room.

Emily won easily.

Then they had to race down the wall.

Emily won easily.

Last of all was the upside-down eight-legged race, right across the ceiling.

Yes, you've guessed, Emily won easily.

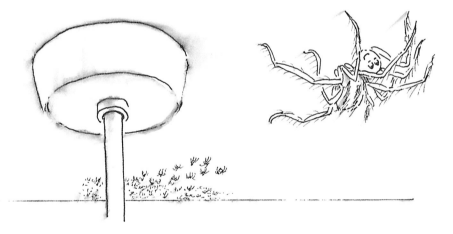

"Amazing!" said all the grown-up spiders.
"Well done, Emily!"

But the spiderlings weren't so happy.

"Why does Emily always win?" they asked one another.

"Why does Emily always win?" they asked the grown-up spiders.

"Because she's the fastest, of course," said the grown-up spiders in the knowing way that old folk have.

"But why is she the fastest?" asked the spiderlings in the annoying way that young folk have. And that was when the truth was discovered.

Emily was asked to appear in front of the Spider Sports Committee to receive her prizes, four neatly parcelled little flies.

"Congratulations, Emily," said the chairperson of the Sports Committee. "You have won all four eight-legged races. Why is that, do you think?"

"If you please," said Emily (for she was by nature a polite spiderling), "it's because I ran the fastest."

"Ah!" said a very old grown-up spider. "But why did you run the fastest?"

Emily scratched her head with her two front legs. "I don't really know," she said modestly. "I suppose I just legged it quicker than they did."

"Legged it?" said the very old grown-up spider.

"Legged it?" said all the other grown-up spiders.

And they all looked carefully at Emily's legs.

They weren't any different from the legs of all the other spiderlings. They were no longer. They were no stronger. They were no hairier. But suddenly they all saw that, though Emily was scratching her head with her two front legs, yet she was still standing on eight others.

Emily had ten legs!

Chapter Two

For a moment nobody spoke.

Then, "Disgraceful!" said the very old grown-up spider.

"Disgusting!" cried the chairperson of the Sports Committee.

"Disqualified!" shouted all the other grown-up spiders.

Then Emily was made to hand back the four neatly parcelled fly-prizes, and the Committee scuttled off to spread the news.

When Mother
Spider heard it, she
went straight up the
wall.

"Egbert!" she
shouted. "Egbert!"
(for that was Father
Spider's name).
"Where are you?"

Father Spider was where he always was,
in the highest darkest corner of the room.

At first he did not answer. His wife
sounded angry. Like most of his kind, he
was a good deal smaller than she was. A
number of his old friends had disappeared,
suddenly and completely, on account of
their wives being angry.

Or hungry.

Or both.

He tensed himself for a quick getaway, and as he saw his large wife approaching, he called out in a syrupy voice, "Why, Muriel," (for that was Mother Spider's name). "Whatever is the matter, dearest?"

"Oh Egbert!" cried Mother Spider. "It's Emily!"

"Who is Emily?"

"One of our children. Oh, the little wretch! Oh the shame! Oh, I'm so embarrassed!"

"Why?"

"She has ten legs," said Mother Spider in a horrified voice.

Now as soon as Father Spider was sure that his wife was not angry with him, he changed his tune completely.

"Look here, Muriel," he said sternly. "First of all, you know that I don't like children. Second, I couldn't care less how many legs they have – she's lucky, this Emily, she's got a couple of spares. And third, I object to being interrupted when I'm busy."

"But you're not doing anything."

"Yes, I am. I'm busy sitting still, waiting for house-flies and bluebottles. Kindly go away!"

Meanwhile Emily sat silent, alone with her thoughts. She had counted her legs carefully, first clockwise, then anti-clockwise, but the answer came out the same either way – ten.

Emily felt sad, as anyone would who had been disqualified and had her prizes taken away and been shouted at by a Sports Committee.

And Mother and Father will be angry too, I suppose, she thought. Grown-ups! They're all the same.

Then she cheered up a bit. At least my brothers and sisters won't care, she thought. I'll go down to the Gym and have some fun. And off she scuttled (very fast, of course).

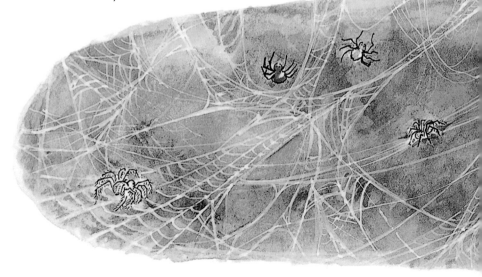

The Gym was an old dusty cupboard, where the spiderlings gathered to practise making their first very small webs, and to do abseiling and climbing and generally enjoy themselves. A number of large disused webs hung across the cupboard, and these acted as safety-nets for those who fell by mistake, and trampolines for those who fell on purpose.

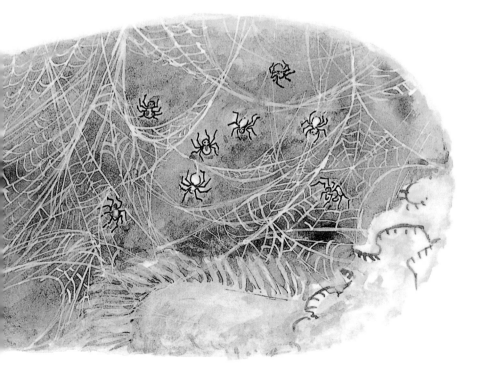

Ten or a dozen spiderlings were in the Gym when Emily arrived, but the moment they saw her, they all stopped doing whatever they were doing and stared at her in silence.

Then one of them spoke.

"Cheat!" it said in a nasty voice. "You're a cheat!"

And then the rest joined in.

"Who's a clever girl then?"

"Won all the races!"

"The eight-legged races!"

"But she's got ten legs!"

"Cheat! Cheat! Dirty cheat!"

"I didn't know." Emily said. "Honest, I didn't know I had ten," but they went on yelling, which made her angry.

"Anyway," she said, "I bet I could beat you lot with two legs tied behind my back."

At this, there was once again silence in the Gym. Then the first spiderling spoke again in a voice that was even nastier.

"You're never going to be given the chance," it said. "Come on, everybody. Get her!"

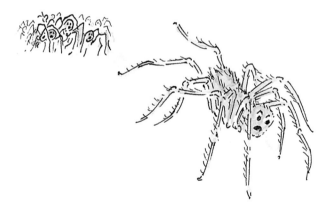

Chapter Three

Emily ran out of the Gym as fast as her ten legs would carry her. She ran down the wall, dashed across the carpet, and hid in a crack in the skirting-board. She waited, facing outwards. The crack was narrow, so that they would only be able to come at her one at a time.

"I'll jolly well show'em," she said to herself. "Calling me a cheat. They'd better be careful."

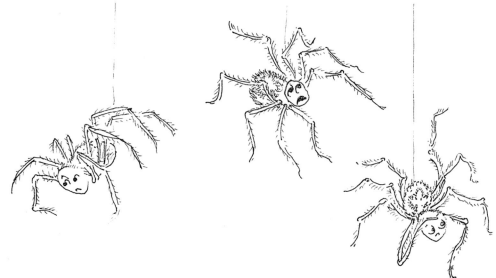

She could hear the spiderlings chattering
to each other as they ran about the room in
search of her.

"Wait till we find her!"

"We'll make her wish she'd never been
hatched!"

"We'll show her!"

"We'll show Miss Emily Ten-legs!"

"Let's pull off one
of them!"

"Let's pull off two!
Then she'd be a
proper spider!"

You just try it, thought Emily. I'm not afraid of you.

But she was, and it was a great relief to hear her mother's voice, calling angrily to the others.

"What are you doing, you naughty children?" she cried to the gang of spiderlings.

"Just playing," they said.

"How many times have I told you not to play out in the room in broad daylight? Stay in the Gym, or under the chairs, or behind the curtains," said Mother Spider.

Then she used the threat that mother spiders everywhere use to frighten their naughty children.

"If you're not careful," she said, "the Hoover will get you! Now scuttle off, the lot of you!"

Emily waited till the spiderlings had gone, and then she came out of her hole. I'd better face the music, she thought. She can't eat me, after all. Or can she?

"Mother?" she said, a little nervously.

Mother Spider was
hanging from the
lampshade. She let out
a thread rapidly and
came whizzing down
to the floor. She did
not look best pleased.
Emily crossed two of
her legs for luck.

Mother Spider
walked all round her
slowly. As she went,
she counted out loud.

"So it's true," she
said at last in a low
voice. "It's true what
they're saying. Never
have I been so
embarrassed."

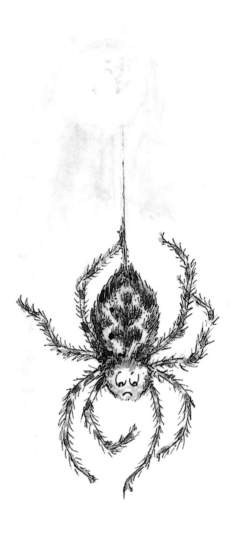

"I didn't know, Mother," said Emily. "Honest, I didn't know I had ten."

"Nor did I," said Mother Spider. "But now that I do, I've only one thing to say to you."

"What's that?"

"Never darken my web again!" said Mother Spider, and she reeled in the thread and shot up into the lampshade without a backward look.

Emily sighed. Perhaps my father will be kinder, she thought. She had never met him, but she knew where he lived.

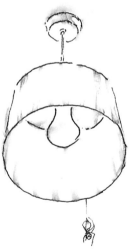

She ran round the
edge of the room,
keeping a sharp eye
out for other spiderlings,
and began to climb
to the highest darkest corner.

Father Spider was busy sitting still when
he felt a slight shudder on his web. He
dashed out, to find, not a house-fly or a
bluebottle, but a
spiderling.

"Father?" said
Emily, a little
nervously.

"Go away!" said
Father Spider crossly.

"You know I don't like children."

"But I'm your daughter."

"I have hundreds of daughters," said Father Spider, "and hundreds of son, and I don't like any of them."

"But I'm Emily."

"The one with ten legs?"

"Yes," said Emily.

"I didn't know, Father," she said. "Honest, I didn't know I had ten."

"What are you moaning about?" said Father Spider. "Think yourself lucky. You've got a couple of spares."

He pulled back the
thread on which
Emily was standing.

"Get lost!" he said,
and he let it go with
a twang.

Emily was hurled
from the web like a
stone from a catapult.

At the same time the room was filled with a sudden roaring noise, a noise that grew louder as Emily fell until, as she hit the floor, it was very loud indeed.

And very close.

Dazed and helpless, Emily could only watch as the monster rushed towards her.

Her mother's words echoed in her brain.

"The Hoover will get you!"

Chapter Four

In time to come, when Emily was herself
a mother spider, her own spiderlings often
asked her for a web-time story. And their
favourite was 'The Day The Hoover Ate
Mum.' They knew, because they had heard
it so often, that it had a happy ending.

But a happy ending was the last thing
Emily expected when she was sucked into
the mouth of the vacuum cleaner.

The first thing she felt was a sharp pain (two sharp pains, to be exact).

Then she found herself in a thick choking blackness, unable to see or to cry out – for her eyes and mouth were full of dust – and unable to hear anything but the dreadful deafening noise of the machine. For a moment, Emily thought she was dead.

But then the Hoover was switched off, the heap of fluff and dirt settled to the bottom of the bag, and Emily fought her way to the top of it.

To her surprise and relief she found she was not alone, for suddenly a voice rang out in the darkness.

"All clear, my lads!" it cried. "Us can unroll now."

Once her eyes had grown accustomed to the darkness, Emily could see that the speaker was a large wood-louse, and that several other wood-lice had climbed to the top of the pile of dust. They looked at Emily in a friendly manner.

"Hullo, young 'un," said the first wood-louse. "You're looking a bit gloomy."

"I am," said Emily. "Nobody likes me. Not my mother nor my father nor my horrid brothers and sisters."

"Whyever not?"

"Because I've got ten legs."

"Poor little mite!" cried the wood-louse. "Only ten!"

"Why d'you say 'only' ten?" said Emily.

"Because you should have fourteen by rights. All wood-lice has fourteen legs."

"But she's not a wood-louse," said a voice behind Emily. "She's a spider."

Emily turned round to see a spiderling, a little smaller than herself, emerging from the dust-pile.

"Who are you?" she said.

"My name's James,"
said the spiderling.
"What's yours?"

"Emily," said Emily.
"I hope you're not
one of my brothers?"

"I hope not," said
James. "They don't sound very nice."

"They're not," said Emily. "They're
horrible to me. And so are my sisters. And
so are my mother and father."

"What are your
parents' names?"
said James.

"Muriel and Egbert."

"Never heard of them."

"Good. Then you
can't be related to me."

"No," said James.

"But when we get out of here, I'd like to be," and he put one of his legs round Emily's waist.

"Oh don't be so soppy!" cried Emily, pushing him away. "Anyway, we're never going to get out of here."

"Oh yes you will, young 'un!" cried the wood-lice.

"All you got to do is wait..."

"... till they empties the Hoover bag..."

"... into the dustbin..."

"... and then you climbs up the inside of it..."

"... and the next time they do take the lid off..."

"... out you pops!"

"But when will they empty it?" said Emily.

"Soon, I should think," said James. "It's pretty full," and hardly were the words out of his mouth when they all felt the Hoover being lifted, and carried away, and set down again.

Then they heard the zip of the outer cover being undone, and the thick paper bag in which they were all imprisoned shook.

"Watch out, my lads!" shouted the first wood-louse. "We'm a-going!"

"Quickly, Emily," said James. "Attach safety-lines!"

He was only just in time, because at that moment the bottom of the paper bag was opened, and dirt and dust and fluff and wood-lice fell into the dustbin.

The bag was empty, save for the two spiderlings suspended within it; and before it could be closed again Emily and James let out thread, swung themselves to the side of the dustbin, and scampered up the wall of it and over the rim and away.

They scuttled for the nearest cover and crouched there breathlessly till all was quiet again.

Then James began to stare at Emily's legs.

Next, he walked all round her slowly. As he went, he counted out loud.

"Oh don't you start!" cried Emily. "If you don't like me having ten legs, you can jolly well push off!"

James stopped at the count of eight.

"You haven't," he said.

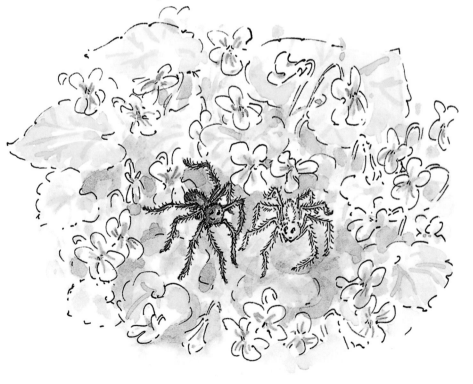

"Haven't what?"

"Haven't got ten legs. You've got eight. Same as any other spider."

And then Emily remembered the sharp pain (two sharp pains, to be exact) as the Hoover had sucked her in.

"Except you're not the same as any other spider, Emily," said James. "You're prettier. I think it would be nice if we set up web together," and once again he put one of his legs round Emily's waist.

"Oh don't be so soppy!" cried Emily. But this time she did not push him away.

44

"And anyway," said James, "they'll grow again."

"What will?"

"The two legs you lost. Spiders of our sort can do that."

"How d'you know?"

"My dad's done it. Mum lost her temper with him one day and pulled off one of his, and he grew a lovely new one."

"Gosh!" said Emily excitedly. "Then I'll still be the fastest spider of them all!"

"Yes."

"But oh!" said Emily miserably. "You won't like me any more, James. Not with ten legs."

"Emily," said James. "When legs are as beautiful as yours, you cannot possibly have too many of them," and he stroked one of hers with one of his.

"Oh James!" said Emily happily. "You say the soppiest things!"

Birdy and the Ghosties
Written by Jill Paton Walsh
Illustrated by Alan Marks

She looked once, and she saw the terrible ghosties…

Sometimes Birdy watches her father row people across the
dangerous sea, but when the wrinkled old woman asks to be
ferried across, Birdy jumps in too. The woman tells Birdy she has
second sight, but Birdy isn't sure she wants this special gift.
However, soon she finds that looking twice at things can bring
the most unexpected results…

Look out for another story from this award-winning team,
also set in Cornwall, *Thomas and the Tinners.*

Fair's Fair
Written by Leon Garfield
Illustrated by Brian Hoskin

"All right," says Jackson. "Fair's fair. Half for you and half for me."

Jackson is cold and starving in the dreadful winter weather. He's
looking forward to the steaming pie that's payment for a long night's
work. When the huge, black dog comes – glaring and growling –
Jackson gives it half his meal. One bargain soon leads to another –
and to unforeseen good fortune…

WAYLAND

These Gripping Tales are short, accessible novels for newly confident readers.

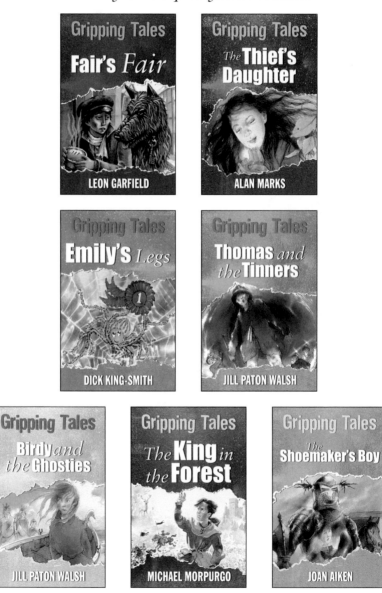

Gripping Tales
Fair's *Fair*
LEON GARFIELD

Gripping Tales
The **Thief's Daughter**
ALAN MARKS

Gripping Tales
Emily's *Legs*
DICK KING-SMITH

Gripping Tales
Thomas *and the* **Tinners**
JILL PATON WALSH

Gripping Tales
Birdy *and the* **Ghosties**
JILL PATON WALSH

Gripping Tales
The **King** *in the* **Forest**
MICHAEL MORPURGO

Gripping Tales
The **Shoemaker's Boy**
JOAN AIKEN